Tinker Bell

Two Pirate Tales

TINKER BELL TAKES CHARGE

AND

IRIDESSA, LOST AT SEA

RANDOM HOUSE 🏠 NEW YORK

All About Fairies

IF YOU HEAD toward the second star on your right and fly straight on till morning, you'll come to Never Land, a magical island where mermaids play and children never grow up.

When you arrive, you might hear something like the tinkling of little bells. Follow that sound and you'll find Pixie Hollow, the secret heart of Never Land.

A great old maple tree grows in Pixie Hollow, and in it live hundreds of fairies and sparrow men. Some of them can do water magic, others can fly like the wind, and still others can speak to animals. You see, Pixie Hollow is the Never fairies' kingdom, and each fairy who lives there has a special, extraordinary talent.

Not far from the Home Tree, nestled in the branches of a hawthorn, is Mother Dove, the most magical creature of all. She sits on her egg, watching over the fairies, who in turn watch over her. For as long as Mother Dove's egg stays well and whole, no one in Never Land will ever grow old.

Once, Mother Dove's egg *was* broken. But we are not telling the story of the egg here. Now it is time for Tinker Bell's and Iridessa's tales. . . .

Tinker Bell Takes Charge

WRITTEN BY
ELEANOR FREMONT

ILLUSTRATED BY
THE DISNEY STORYBOOK ARTISTS

RANDOM HOUSE 🏠 NEW YORK

IT WAS A MILD, sunny day in Pixie Hollow—a perfect sort of a day. Little white clouds scampered across a dazzling blue sky. A soft breeze rustled the leaves of the Home Tree, the great ageless maple where the Never fairies lived.

Although it was a perfect day, Tinker Bell was not in her usual high spirits. Something was bothering her, but she could not figure out what it was. She wasn't sick. She wasn't sad. It was more like she had an itch that she couldn't find, let alone scratch.

Just that morning, she had caught sight of her face in the polished walls of the Home Tree's lobby. She'd noticed her slumped shoulders and the frown on her face. Even her ponytail drooped.

This troublesome feeling was on her mind now as she flew toward her bedroom, which was high in the branches of the Home Tree. She needed to change her shoes before she could go back to her workshop. The ones she was wearing had gotten soaked on a visit to Thistle's strawberry patch. Thistle, a garden-talent fairy, had asked Tink to look at a garden hoe that needed fixing. It had been left on the damp ground among the strawberries, and the blade had rusted through. It would have to be replaced. *But it will be easy to fix*, Tink thought.

She headed up through the trunk of the Home Tree. The trunk split into branches. She turned right, then left, then left again, winding upward. The corridor narrowed as the tree's limbs tapered.

Tink's bedroom was at the end of one of the topmost branches. When the hallway was so tight that her head nearly grazed the ceiling, she reached the door to her room.

As soon as she was inside, her spirits lifted a bit. Tink loved her room. Everything in it reflected her talent and personality. There was her beloved bed, which was made from a pirate's metal loaf pan. There were the lampshades made from old colanders. Even the chair she was sitting on was special. The back of it was made from a serving platter, the seat was a frying pan, and the legs were made from old serving spoons.

At one point or another, Tink had repaired the frying pan, the platter, and each of the spoons. Some she had repaired more than once. But eventually, pans and spoons wore out. Although Tink thought anything broken could be fixed, the kitchen-talent fairies didn't always agree. Sometimes they threw their worn-out pots and platters away.

Tink felt a special connection with every pot and pan she'd ever fixed. She couldn't bear to see any of them on the scrap-metal heap. So when the kitchen-talent fairies had thrown out the pan, the platter, and the spoons, she'd rescued them and brought them back to her workshop. With a lot of thought and a few pinches of fairy dust, she'd turned them into a chair.

Tink thought about the frying-pan chair as she closed the door to her room and flew back down through the Home Tree. What a wonderful challenge it had been to make. Not like fixing Thistle's silly rusted hoe. There was nothing hard about replacing a hoe blade. No challenge at all.

Suddenly Tink stopped in her tracks.

"That's it!" she said aloud. "That is what's bothering me! No challenge!"

Tink was one of the best pots-and-pans-talent fairies in all of Pixie Hollow. Her joy came from fixing things. She liked a challenging problem more than almost anything.

But for weeks now, every job Tink had been given had been as easy as gooseberry pie. No pots that wouldn't boil water. No colanders that refused to drain. No pans that were more hole than pan. Just "fix this little hole, fix that little hole." Boring, boring, boring.

But at least now I know what's wrong, Tink thought. *What I need is a problem to solve! A big one!*

"Tink!" A voice behind her interrupted her thoughts. Tink turned. Her good friend Rani, a water-talent fairy, was hurrying toward her.

Being the only fairy without wings, Rani could not fly. So Tink gently landed on the moss carpet in the Home Tree's hallway. She waited until Rani caught up.

"Where are you going?" Rani asked.

"I was just on my way back to my workshop," Tink replied. "Why do you—"

"Ask?" said Rani. She had a habit of finishing everyone's sentences. "No big reason. I just thought maybe we could play a game of—"

But Rani never got to finish. At that moment, she was interrupted by a tremendous crash. Both fairies heard branches cracking and snapping near the top of the Home Tree.

In the next instant, there was a *thud* that shook the tree to its very roots. Tink and Rani nearly lost their balance. From the nearby tearoom came the sound of dishes falling and shattering.

Then there was silence.

Tink and Rani stared at each other.

"Did the moon just fall out of the sky?" Rani whispered in awe.

"Maybe it was a branch falling from another tree," said Tink. But even as she spoke, she knew that wasn't it. The sound had been made by something very heavy and solid. And it had landed quite close by.

"Maybe a great big bird just came in for a landing," said Rani.

"Maybe," said Tink. But that didn't seem right either.

The two fairies listened carefully. After a long moment Tink took a deep breath and straightened her shoulders. "We've got to go and see—"

"What it is. If you say so," said Rani. She dabbed her forehead with a leafkerchief and attempted to smile bravely. Though they were both nervous, it was a lot easier to see it on Rani. She was the most watery of all the water-talent fairies. At the moment, her forehead was beaded with sweat.

The two fairies headed back toward the front entrance of the Home Tree. Tink walked so that she wouldn't get too far ahead of Rani. Brave as she was, even Tink didn't want to go outside alone. Together they hurried past the tearoom, down the corridor, through the lobby, and out the knothole door.

When Tink stepped into the sunlight, she stopped cold and gasped. Rani, who was right on Tink's heels, crashed into her.

Rani peeked over Tink's shoulder. She gasped, too.

"*What* is *that?*" she whispered.

2

RIGHT IN FRONT of them was a huge, menacing-looking black ball. It was taller than two fairies put together and just as wide. It had landed right in the middle of the Home Tree's courtyard.

A large crack ran through the courtyard where it had smashed down. Several toadstool chairs had been damaged or squashed completely. The ground around the ball was covered with the splintered remains of branches and twigs.

Tink's mind reeled. The courtyard was a very special place for the fairies. Many of their most important meetings and celebrations were held there. Not to mention, the fairies had to fly through it to reach the Home Tree's knothole door.

Whenever Tink saw the courtyard, she felt that she was home. It always seemed to say, "Welcome. The Home Tree waits to embrace you." Now the sight of the damaged courtyard made her heart ache.

A large crowd of fairies had gathered around the ball. Clarion, the fairy queen, stepped forward.

"Is everyone all right?" she asked.

Her voice was tense with worry. "Is anyone hurt?"

Noses and wings were quickly counted, amid a buzz of concern. Incredibly, every fairy in the Home Tree had escaped harm.

The queen sighed with relief. She looked around the crowd. "Terence, Spring, Jerome, Rosetta, Luna," she said. Her voice had regained its normal regal tone. The fairies and sparrow men sprang to attention. "Fly to the top of the tree and see what damage has been done. Please report back at once."

With Terence, a fairy-dust-talent sparrow man, in the lead, the group took off.

When they had gone, a scullery-talent fairy tiptoed up to the great ball. She raised her hand as if to touch its rough surface. But at the last second she pulled her hand back. "Do you think it might be alive?" she whispered.

All at once, the fairies nearest to the ball hopped back a couple of steps.

"What's it made of?" asked Dulcie, a baking-talent fairy.

The fairies around her shook their heads, muttering, "Don't know."

"Maybe it's a big rock," said Angus, a pots-and-pans-talent sparrow man. "Though I've certainly never seen a rock this round before."

"Maybe it's a giant black pearl," said Rani. "Though I've never seen a pearl this big."

Tink shook her head. "No," she said. "It would be shiny if it were a pearl."

Dulcie flew hesitantly up to it. She gave it a small rap with her knuckles. "Ow!" she said. "It's hard!" She blew on her hand. "And it's hot!" she added.

Tink didn't like to stand around. And she had stood around long enough. Bravely, she marched up to the ball and gave it a good hard smack.

"It's iron," she said. She shook her hand to cool it off from the hot metal. "Good old-fashioned Never iron."

Several fairies frowned. "Iron is really heavy," Dulcie said worriedly.

"It's going to be hard to move," said Rani. She started to cry.

"We should try to find out where it

came from," the queen told them. "That might help us figure out how to get rid of it."

Her suggestion was greeted with enthusiasm. "Let's take a good look at it," said Rani. She wiped the tears from her eyes.

The fairies all moved in closer. They circled the ball. Some fairies flew around the top. Others bent down low to look at the part that touched the ground.

"Hold on!" said Tink. She hovered like a hummingbird near the very top of the ball. "I see something."

Other fairies flew over to join her. "You're right," said Lily, a garden-talent fairy. "It's some kind of a mark."

Angus nodded. "It's almost like a—"

"A hook!" Tink shouted in triumph. "It's a mark that looks like a hook! And you know what that means."

"*Captain Hook!*" cried several fairies.

"Of course. Why didn't I realize it before? It's a cannonball!" Tink declared.

Tink had seen plenty of cannonballs back in the days when she had spent all her time with Peter Pan. But she had never before seen a cannonball in Pixie Hollow. Hook and his pirates never came to this part of Never Land's forest. And the fairies tried to avoid the pirates as much as they could.

Just then, they heard a muffled boom from the direction of Pirate Cove. Several fairies jumped.

"Cannon fire," said Queen Clarion. "Captain Hook must be after Peter Pan again."

The others knew what she meant. On Never Land, there was an on-and-off battle between Hook and his pirates and Peter and the Lost Boys. On certain quiet nights, when the wind was just right, the fairies could hear Pan and Hook's swords clashing in the distance.

"Hmm," said Tink with a worried little frown. Peter Pan was a friend of Tink's. Though she rarely saw him anymore, she knew him better than any of the other fairies did. She didn't like to think of Captain Hook firing cannonballs at Peter.

But Peter is too quick and too clever to get hit by a cannonball, Tink assured herself.

There was another muffled boom, followed by a whizzing sound.

"Everyone, duck!" said the queen.

The fairies all dashed for cover in the roots of the Home Tree. Something flew through the air high over their heads. It landed in the nearby forest with a tremendous thud.

"The fairy circle!" cried Dulcie. She hurried out from behind a root. "What if it landed there?"

"What about Mother Dove?" Rani said, almost in a whisper. "What if it hit her hawthorn tree?"

The fairies looked at each other in stricken silence. Mother Dove was the closest thing to pure goodness in all of Never Land. She was the source of all the fairies' magic. They had almost lost her once, when a hurricane hit Never Land. The thought of losing her again was too dreadful to bear.

In a tense voice, Queen Clarion told

several fast-flying fairies to fly to the hawthorn and check on Mother Dove. They zipped off in a blur.

Moments later, the fast fliers were back.

"Mother Dove is fine," a fast-flying sparrow man reported. "Not one feather ruffled. And the fairy circle is undamaged."

The fairies let out a collective sigh of relief.

Tink glared at the big black cannonball in the courtyard. "How dare those pirates!" she exclaimed. "How could they be so careless? I say—"

But before she could say more, Spring, a message-talent fairy, came speeding up to her. She had a grim look on her face.

"Tink," she said. "I've just been to the top of the Home Tree. I think you'd better come with me."

3

WHAT NOW? Tink wondered. *And what does it have to do with me?*

Maybe something metal has broken, and they need me to fix it, Tink mused. *But why right at this moment?*

She followed the messenger into the Home Tree. They passed through the main corridor, where paintings repre-senting each different Never fairy talent hung on the walls. Tink saw that most of the paintings were crooked. Some had even fallen to the floor. She stopped and straightened the painting of a dented stewpot, which was the symbol for the pots-and-pans talent.

Up through the branches they went. They turned right, then left, then left again. Finally, they came to the corridor that led to Tink's room. Tink saw her friend Terence waiting for her. Terence had been in the group the queen had sent to check the damage to the tree. He looked upset.

"Tink," he said, "I hardly know how to tell you this. Your bedroom—"

Her beloved bedroom! Tink didn't even wait for him to finish his sentence.

She zoomed down the corridor to the end of the branch where her room sat. What would she find? she wondered. Would it be a horrible mess? Would her loaf-pan bed be overturned, or even dented? It was not a pleasant thought.

When she reached the tip of the branch, she stopped cold.

Her room wasn't a mess. Her room wasn't there at all.

Tinker Bell hovered, staring. The walls, the ceiling, and everything in the room had disappeared. All that remained was the floor and the jagged edges of the broken walls.

She looked up past the hole where her ceiling should have been. The surrounding branches had a few broken twigs. But the other fairies' rooms were

still there. The cannonball had hit Tink's room, and Tink's alone.

Tink felt faint. She sat down cross-legged on the floor.

How could my room just be . . . gone? she thought. *Where will I sleep? Where will I keep my clothes and other things? Where are my clothes and other things?*

More fairies began to arrive to see what had happened.

"Oh, Tink," said her friend Beck. "It's awful!"

"I can't believe it," said Prilla. "Your bed is gone. And it was such a great bed."

Tink stood up. She didn't want the other fairies to feel sorry for her. She took a deep breath. "We'll just rebuild it," she said. She sounded calmer than she felt. "And it will be an even better room than before."

"We'll all help you," said Terence. The others nodded in agreement.

Suddenly Tink felt angry. After all, no one would have to rebuild anything if it weren't for the cannonball. Her hands balled into tiny fists thinking about it.

"And in the meantime," she said fiercely, "we're going to get that horrid cannonball out of our courtyard. What do you say, fairies?"

"Yes!" they all cried. "Let's do it!"

With Tink in the lead, the fairies went back to the courtyard. The most obvious thing was to try pushing the cannonball,

Tink decided. "If a lot of us get behind it and fly as hard as we can, maybe we can roll it out of the courtyard," she said.

"Let's move every little twig out of its path. That way it won't get stuck on anything," said Beck.

The cleaning-talent fairies grabbed their brooms and swept up all the splinters. Other fairies helped by moving the pieces of the squashed mushroom chairs.

"All right," said Tink. "Let's get into pushing formation."

Several fairies arranged themselves behind the ball. The strongest ones hovered close to the bottom. The weaker ones stayed near the top.

"One, two, three . . . *shove!*" shouted Tink.

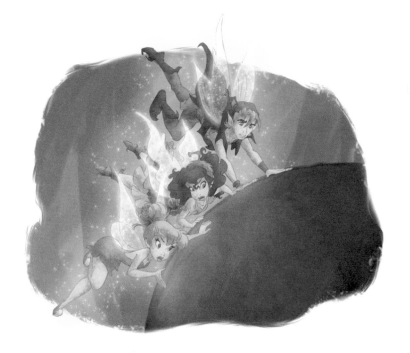

The fairies beat their wings madly. They heaved against the ball as hard as they could.

After a moment, they stopped. Several fairies leaned against the ball, panting.

"I think it moved a tiny, tiny bit," said Prilla, who was inclined to see the best in all situations.

"It didn't move an inch," said Angus, who was not.

"Let's give it another try," said Tink.

They rearranged themselves. Now the strongest fairies went to the top of the ball. The weaker ones went to the bottom.

"One, two, three . . . *shove!*" Tink cried again.

The fairies used every ounce of strength they had. At last they stopped. Their wings were quivering with exhaustion.

"Nothing," said Angus.

Indeed, the ball had not moved, not a hair.

Tink sighed. "Well, I guess that's not going to work," she said. "But this is only the beginning."

4

As the other fairies sat down to rest, Tink began to pace. She was sure she could come up with an idea that would work. She tugged at her bangs, thinking hard.

Down in the meadow near the dairy barn, the faint sound of bells could be heard. Cannonball or no cannonball, the dairy mice had to be fed. The mouse-herding-talent fairies were taking the herd out to pasture.

Tink looked toward the meadow. "Mice!" she said suddenly.

"Mice?" said two of the fairies nearest to her.

"Yes," said Tink. "Mice. It's simple. We'll harness all the dairy mice to the cannonball. Maybe, together, all of them can move it!"

"Wonderful idea, Tink!" said Queen Clarion.

The messenger-talent fairies headed for the pasture to tell the mouse-herding fairies to round up the dairy mice. Meanwhile, the kitchen-talent fairies hurried back to the kitchen to collect all the loaves of acorn bread they could

spare. The mice adored acorn bread. Occasionally, a mouse would get loose from the herd and be caught in the Home Tree pantry, nibbling bread. Now the fairies could use the bread as a lure to get the mice to pull the ball.

Fairies from other talents pitched in too. Florian and the rest of the weaving-talent fairies quickly fashioned ropes from sweet grass they'd plucked from the meadow.

"I wish we had time to collect marsh grass," Florian said. "It makes a stronger rope. But I think this should do."

It only took a few minutes for the mouse-herders to get the mice to the Home Tree. One by one, the fairies began to harness the mice to the rope. All together, there were thirty-six mice. They stood at attention, their noses quivering.

At last, they were all in formation. The mouse-herding fairies stood just in front of them, waving the bread. The mice squeaked excitedly at the sight and smell of it.

"That's it, my little loves," said one

of the mouse herders. "Delicious bread! Come and get it."

She stepped back a little. The mice strained toward her. "Come on," the fairy urged. "Acorn bread! More than you've ever had before. You can have it all if you just try!"

And the mice did try. They loved that bread more than anything, much more than the sweetgrass seeds they were usually fed. They strained toward the bread. Their little claws dug into the ground. The courtyard echoed with the sounds of their squeaking.

The other fairies cheered them on. "You can do it, mice!" they yelled. "Get the bread! Move the ball! You can do it!"

The ball wobbled. The mice leaned into their harnesses—and the ball moved. Not a lot, maybe half an inch. But it moved.

"It's working, Tink!" cried Terence. He gave her an enormous smile and clapped her on the back.

"It's working! It's working!" other fairies echoed.

Tink's face was flushed. Her eyes shone. All her attention was focused on the cannonball. It moved another half inch, and—

Snap!

The rope around the cannonball broke. The mice leaped forward, suddenly free from the weight. They lunged at the bread in the mouse-herders' hands and quickly began to gobble it down.

The fairies stopped in mid-cheer. Everyone let out a disappointed sigh.

"Marsh grass," said Florian. She shook her head. "It always makes a stronger rope."

Tink flew over to look at the mice. They were still panting from the effort of pulling the ball. Their furry sides heaved in and out.

"Do you think they could do it again?" she asked one of the mouse-herding fairies. "If we made a stronger rope, that is."

The fairy shook her head. "I don't think so," she said. "It might wear them out. Dairy mice can be quite delicate, you know. If they get too tired, they stop giving milk."

Tink's shoulders slumped. But she tried hard not to show her disappointment. "Well," she said, "it was a good try. We'll just have to think of something else."

Queen Clarion spoke up. "Maybe that's enough work for one day," she said gently. "The cannonball won't go anywhere before tomorrow. Why don't we all get cleaned up and have some dinner?"

The fairies murmured their agreement. Not only were they all tired, they were also very hungry.

As the other fairies headed into the Home Tree, Tink lingered behind.

Well, Tink, you wanted a challenge,

she said to herself. *And now you've got one.*

She stared up at the huge cannon-ball. *But am I up to it?* she wondered.

5

BECAUSE THE KITCHEN was such a mess, dinner that night was simple—acorn-butter sandwiches with dandelion salad. The tired fairies ate quickly. The sun had already set. After a long, hard day of work, they were eager to go to bed.

As soon as she was done eating, Tink realized she had a problem. She had nowhere to sleep. She watched as the other fairies headed for their rooms. In all the excitement over the cannonball, they had forgotten that Tink didn't have her own room to go to.

The tearoom slowly emptied. Tink remained sitting at her table. She wasn't sure what to do. As the shadows lengthened, she felt more and more forlorn.

At last Rani noticed Tink sitting alone. She realized the problem at once.

"Tink," she said, "what will you do tonight?"

"I think maybe I'll just sleep outside," Tink replied bravely. "I can use a maple leaf as a blanket."

"You can sleep in my room," Rani told her. "It's better than sleeping outside, anyway."

"Okay," Tink said. She felt relieved. "I would like that. I'm awfully tired."

Tink followed Rani up to her room. She had visited Rani's room many times before. But until that evening, she hadn't noticed the details. She looked around at the blue-green walls and the seaweed curtains hanging in the windows. The floor was paved with smooth river stones.

It seemed like a quiet, peaceful place. Tink was looking forward to a good night's sleep.

"Shall we play a game of seashell tiddlywinks?" Rani asked.

"Not tonight," said Tink. She really was exhausted. "I think I'm ready to go to bed. Where should I sleep?"

"I could pile lots of blankets on the floor," Rani suggested.

"Let me help you," said Tink.

Together they piled woven-fern blankets on the floor until they had made a soft bed.

"That should be very comfortable," Tink said when they were done. But she could not help noticing how humid Rani's room was. Even the blankets felt damp.

Tink settled herself on the pile. She was so tired, she was sure she'd fall asleep in a moment.

Rani covered her up with a sheet, which was also slightly damp. "Good night, dear friend," she said. Then she climbed into her own bed, which was made from driftwood. She pulled the seaweed quilt up to her chin.

Tink lay on her back, gazing at the blue-green ceiling. *It was nice of Rani to take me in*, she thought. Then she closed her eyes and gave in to her tiredness.

Seconds later, Tink opened her eyes. She could feel a lump beneath the pile of blankets. It was one of the river stones that paved the floor.

Tink tried turning on her side, but that was no better. She flopped over on her stomach, but that was worse still. She ended up on her back again.

Tink thought wistfully of her comfy loaf-pan bed and the soft, dappled light that came through the colander lamp-shades in her room. How she loved to fall asleep beneath the still life of the stockpot, whisk, and griddle. And now it was gone, all gone. Tink sighed.

Moonlight filtered in through the seaweed curtains. Suddenly Tink gasped and jumped up. Two long arms seemed to reach out to her from the corner of the room.

Rani heard her and sat straight up. "What's the matter?" she cried.

"Th-there's something in the corner!" whispered Tink. She was almost too scared to breathe.

"Where? I don't see it!" whispered Rani. She followed the direction of Tink's pointing finger. But the room was too dark. They couldn't see clearly.

Quickly, Rani lit her scallop-shell lamp. Then she started to giggle. "That's just my clothes hanging on a clothes tree, Tink. It's made from a coral branch. Remember?"

Gradually, Tink's heart stopped racing. Her breath returned to normal. "Oh," she said. "So it is." Now she felt foolish. She wished more than ever that she could be in her own bed.

Rani turned out the light. They settled back down to sleep.

Tink tried to drift off, she really did. But the paving rocks were not getting any softer. And then she became aware of another thing.

Drip. Drip. Drip-drip. Drip.
Drip. Drip. Drip-drip. Drip.

It was a slow, steady rhythm. Tink had forgotten all about Rani's drip. She had a permanent leak in her room, whether it was raining or not. Beneath the leak sat a bucket made from a human-sized thimble. Inside the bucket, a Never minnow swam contentedly around and around.

Drip. Drip. Drip-drip. Drip.

By now, Tink had given up trying to sleep. She lay on her back and stared at the ceiling. Every now and then she shifted her wings under the damp sheet to find a better position.

Sometime before dawn, Tink heard a new noise. It was Rani crying.

"Rani," whispered Tink, "are you all right?"

There was no answer, just more crying. Tink brightened her glow so she could see Rani a little better. Rani was sound asleep, weeping onto her pillow. The air in the room was getting damper and damper.

"Rani," Tink tried again. "Wake up. You're having a bad dream."

Still Rani did not wake. Tink finally gave up and went back to staring at the ceiling. She listened to the dripping water and Rani's crying.

A little after dawn, Rani awoke. She sat up in bed and stretched her arms toward the ceiling. "I just had the most wonderful dream!" she said when she saw that Tink was awake.

"No, you didn't. You had an awful

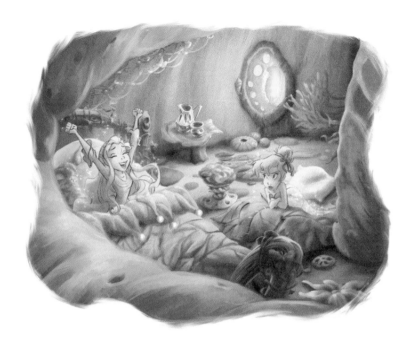

dream," Tink snapped. She was fairly
cross, having not slept a wink the whole
night.

Rani gave her a strange look and
shook her head. "No, it was long and
wonderful," she said. "I was playing with
a big ball of water. I was tossing it back

and forth with Silvermist and Tally. We could throw it as high as the top of the Home Tree and make a rainbow in the sunlight. It was so beautiful!"

Now it was Tink's turn to give Rani a strange look. "But you were crying," she insisted. "Cupfuls. Buckets. Barrels. Feel your bed, it's all—"

Rani broke into a big grin. "—wet," she finished. "I was crying in the dream, too! Crying from happiness!"

Tink just shook her head. She got up from her damp, lumpy bed. "Rani," she said, "you are my very good friend. But I am a pots-and-pans fairy and you are a water fairy, and I will never truly understand you." She smiled and gave Rani a hug.

Rani's eyes filled with tears again. "You're my good friend, too. And I'll never really understand you, either," she said, hugging Tink back. She wiped her eyes with a leafkerchief. "Do you want to go have some breakfast?"

"Yes," said Tink. "But my wings are too damp to fly."

Rani picked up another leafkerchief and gently dried Tink's wings. Then they went downstairs for breakfast.

6

Breakfast was very good, as usual.
Platters of Dulcie's wonderful pumpkin
muffins and pots of blackberry tea sat
on every table in the tearoom. But no
breakfast would have been delicious
enough to cheer Tink up that morning.

Tink was tired. She was damp. And
she wanted her room back.

She stared gloomily at the serving

platter in front of her. It reminded her of her platter–frying-pan–spoon chair.

"Rough night?" asked Angus. He was sitting next to Tink at the pots-and-pans-talent table.

"Just a little damp," said Tink with a sigh. She took a sip of tea. "But don't worry. I'm ready to get to work. I'll have that cannonball out of Pixie Hollow in no time." Even to her own ears, she did not sound very sure.

"Tinker Bell!" a cheerful voice exclaimed. Tink turned around. Gwinn, a tiny decoration-talent fairy, was beaming at her. "Are you ready to start putting your room back together?" Gwinn asked. "Cedar and I are heading up there now to get started." She gestured at

Cedar, who was standing behind her.

Cedar was the biggest, strongest-looking fairy Tinker Bell had ever seen. She was nearly six inches tall! It was clear from the hammer and saw Cedar was carrying that she was a carpenter-talent fairy.

Cedar nodded shyly in greeting. Her great height made Gwinn look even tinier.

"Usually, we prepare rooms for fairies who have just arrived in Never Land," Gwinn continued. She spoke very, very fast. Tink had to concentrate to keep up. "Of course, we don't know them yet. So we just make our best guess about what that fairy might want. And then we hope she likes it. But you're already *here*! I've never helped a fairy decorate her own room before! You can tell me exactly what you want! It will be perfect! *Perfect!* Right, Cedar?"

Cedar nodded and stared bashfully at the ground.

Tink bit her lip. She wanted to start

rebuilding her room. But she had promised to get rid of the cannonball.

Angus read her mind. "You can work on the cannonball later, Tink, after you and Gwinn decide what your new room should look like," he pointed out.

Tink thought about it for a moment. Angus was right. The cannonball could wait.

"All right," Tink said. She smiled. "Let's go!"

A short time later, Tink was watching Cedar hammer planks into the walls of her new room.

Gwinn flew from one corner to the next, measuring the space with her eyes.

She kept up a steady stream of chatter.

"You'll want silver paint," Gwinn told Tink. "Or maybe gold. Or something copper? Ooh, yes! Copper could be just lovely with the sunlight coming in—"

"Silver will be fine," said Tink, trying to keep up.

"And I suppose you'd like colander lampshades again," Gwinn went on. "Although a nice iris-petal lantern would give the room a softer look. . . ."

"Colanders, please," Tink cut in. She was surprised to find she was having fun.

"And you'll need curtains, a bedspread, some kind of rug. . . ." Gwinn zipped from corner to corner. She was making Tink dizzy.

Tink sat down in the middle of the bare floor to watch her.

Gwinn will make sure that the walls are the right color, Tink thought. *And she will get new colanders for the lamps.* But Gwinn couldn't make her another still-life painting. And Cedar couldn't make her another loaf-pan bed.

If I want my room back just the way it was, Tink thought, *I'm going to have to take matters into my own hands.*

"I'll be back in a little while," she told Gwinn and Cedar.

Cedar mumbled good-bye through a mouthful of nails. Gwinn absent-mindedly waved some curtain fabric at her. Tink flew out through the open ceiling and over the woods of Pixie Hollow.

Soon, Tink arrived at Bess's studio. It was made from an old tangerine crate that the art-talent fairy had set up in a remote clearing in the woods, where she could paint in peace and quiet.

Tink found Bess hard at work. She was painting a portrait of an animal-talent fairy. The animal-talent fairy posed on a cushion, holding her favorite ladybug on her lap.

"Tink!" Bess said. She set down her brush and hugged her friend. "What a terrible thing to happen to your room. Is there anything I can do to help?"

"Actually, there is," said Tink. She explained that she needed another still life of a stockpot, whisk, and griddle to hang over her bed.

Bess looked a little embarrassed. "Oh, Tink," she said unhappily. "Of *course* I'll paint a new picture for you. But I won't be able to get to it for a while. I've already promised paintings to five other fairies."

The animal-talent fairy cleared her throat impatiently. The ladybug on her lap was getting restless. Bess gave Tink another hug, and then got back to work.

Tink flew off, trying not to feel discouraged. Her next stop was the kitchen. She hoped to find some pots and pans that were beyond repair. With luck, she could make another frying-pan chair exactly like her old one.

Dulcie met Tink at the kitchen door. She was carrying a tray of pretty little tea

cakes. As Dulcie set the cakes on a windowsill to cool, Tink asked her if she had any pots, pans, spoons, whisks, or other kitchen items that she needed to get rid of.

"Well," replied Dulcie, "there was that salad fork with the bent tines. I was ready to give up on it. But Angus fixed it last week. It's been perfectly pointy and prongy ever since."

The other pots-and-pans fairies are too good at their jobs, Tink thought. She tugged at her bangs and gave a frustrated sigh. She didn't want to make a chair out of objects that were still useful.

Tink could usually fix almost anything. But here was something that couldn't be fixed, at least not right away.

"Grrr!" cried Tink. She shot three inches into the air with sheer frustration. Her room was smashed, and even when it was fixed, it still wouldn't feel like her room. After all, *where* was she going to find another loaf-pan bed?

That cannonball will regret the day it fell into Pixie Hollow, Tink vowed. *And Captain Hook will regret it even more.*

7

TINK ZOOMED into the courtyard. She flew right up to the cannonball and gave it a mighty kick.

Ow! Tink danced through the air, clutching her toes and grimacing in pain. A few fairies who had been flying by stared at Tink in astonishment.

Once her toes stopped hurting, Tink found that she felt much calmer. But now she was more determined than ever to get rid of the big, bad ball.

"This cannonball is going to move!" she cried. "I am going to banish it from Pixie Hollow once and for all. But I'm going to need help from every fairy and sparrow man. Together, we can do it! Now, who's with me?"

But the other fairies didn't jump up as Tink hoped they would.

"I don't know. Maybe we could learn to live with the cannonball," said one of the decoration-talent fairies. "We could probably fix it up to make it look nice."

The other decoration-talent fairies brightened a bit. "We could!" one agreed. "We could decorate it with hollyhock garlands and daisy chains."

"Or we could paint it a pretty shade of green to sort of blend in," said another. "Maybe a nice sage color."

"But . . . but don't you want to get rid of it?" Tink asked, astonished.

"Well, of course we do, Tink," said Beck, who happened to be in the courtyard. "But we want to get back to doing what we usually do. We're all busy with our own talents."

Tink couldn't believe what she was hearing. Were the other fairies giving up already, before they'd even tried?

"We have fun in the courtyard, don't we?" she said. "It's part of our home. How will we feel looking at this cannonball every time we come out of the Home Tree? We'll never be able to

have a meeting or a party here again.
Even if it's decorated and painted, it will
still take up too much room."

Several fairies murmured in agreement. But no one volunteered to help.

"We tried moving it yesterday, and
we couldn't," a water-talent sparrow
man pointed out.

"I know we can do this," Tink
replied. "We just have to figure out how."

Just then, Terence flew up. He was
holding a teacup in one hand. In his
other hand was a sack of fairy dust.

"Tink, you didn't get your fairy dust
yet today, did you?" he said.

As a dust-talent sparrow man,
Terence handed out dust to all the fairies
and sparrow men in Pixie Hollow.

Everyone got one teacupful per day. The dust was what allowed the fairies to fly and do magic.

As Terence poured the magical dust over Tink, her eyes widened. "That's it! I know how we can move the cannonball!" she cried.

The fairies in the courtyard perked up. "How, Tink?" Terence asked.

"We move big things with balloon carriers, right?" Tink said. Balloon carriers were baskets attached to fairy-dust-filled balloons. The fairies used them to move things that were too heavy to carry. "That's what we'll do with the cannonball. We'll build a giant balloon and use lots of extra fairy dust to give it more lift. We can float the cannonball away."

"It's a good idea," said Terence. The other fairies nodded. Even Angus looked impressed.

"Send word to the other dust-talent fairies," Tink told Terence. "We'll need all the fairy dust they can spare. The rest of us will get the balloon carrier ready."

This was easier said than done. In order to attach the balloon to the cannonball, they would need heavy ropes. Tink found Florian and explained her plan.

"We'll use marsh grass this time," Florian said with certainty. "And we'll make it extra thick."

She got the weaving-talent fairies together, and they set out to collect long strands of tough marsh grasses, which they would weave into the strongest ropes they could make.

Next, Tink went to the sewing-talent fairies. She asked them to make a silk balloon, the biggest one Pixie Hollow had ever seen.

Some of the fairies grumbled. They didn't want to leave the pretty petal dresses and leaf-frock coats they were working on. But Tink's spirit was catching.

Soon, they were collecting every spare scrap of spider silk to make the giant balloon.

It was afternoon by the time the weaving-talent fairies finished making the ropes. But they looked sturdy this time. They were nearly as thick as a fairy's waist.

The weavers secured the ropes around the bottom of the cannonball. Then it was time to attach the balloon. The sewing-talent fairies sewed the ends of each rope to the edges of the balloon.

Tink oversaw all this work. She paced back and forth, worrying. Would the balloon lift off? Would the cannonball stay attached? What if this idea didn't work either?

At last, the whole contraption was ready to go. It was time for the dust-talent fairies and sparrow men to do their work.

By now a crowd had gathered. Everyone watched, hardly daring to breathe, as Terence and a dust-talent sparrow man named Jerome began to fill the balloon with fairy dust. Instead of the teacups they usually used to hand out the dust, they scooped up great mounds of it with shovels they had borrowed from the garden-talent fairies.

The balloon started to rise—up, up, up. The fairies watched in wonder. Soon the balloon was completely inflated. It strained against the ropes.

The ropes pulled taut, but the

cannonball stayed stubbornly on the ground.

"More fairy dust!" cried Tink.

Terence and Jerome flew up to the top of the balloon and sprinkled more shovelfuls of dust onto it. They sprinkled some dust onto the cannonball for good measure. The balloon strained harder and harder. All the fairies and sparrow men strained with it. Their muscles were tense. Their wings vibrated in sheer concentration. The fairies glowed brightly as they willed the balloon to rise.

And finally, it did! The grass ropes pulled tauter, and the cannonball could resist no longer. It lifted off the ground.

"It's going!" shouted Tink.

First it rose just a hair off the ground, no more than the thickness of a fairy's wing. Then it reached the height of two hairs. Then it was almost as high up as a fairy's knee, and then higher than a fairy's head. It was working! It was really working!

If the fairies and sparrow men had not been so caught up in the progress of the cannonball, they might have noticed that a strong breeze had sprung up. But they did not notice, until—

Pow!

Hisssssss.

"What was that?" Tink cried in alarm.

What it was, they soon discovered, was a horse chestnut. The spiky green globe had fallen from a nearby horse chestnut tree. And the wind had been blowing in just the right direction to push it into the balloon. The horse chestnut's spikes had pierced the delicate spider silk.

The hissing lasted only a second. The cannonball landed back in the courtyard with a great thud. Inside the tree, delicate cups and saucers could be heard shattering in the tearoom.

The fairies groaned.

"Well, that's the end of that," Angus said.

But that wasn't the end. For the cannonball had gotten just the start it needed. It began to roll.

8

"THE BALL!" Rani cried. "L-look out!"

Several fairies leaped out of the way
in the nick of time. There was a very
slight slope away from the Home Tree,
but that was enough. The cannonball
rolled down it.

"Hooray!" a decoration-talent fairy
yelled. "Good-bye, ball!"

"Good riddance!" added a butterfly

herder. Other fairies joined in the cheering.

But Tink followed the ball's progress, frowning.

"It's great that we got it going, but—" she began.

"Now we don't know *where* it's going," Rani finished for her.

"Exactly," said Tink.

The ball began to pick up speed. The fairies' cheers died out.

"It was so hard to start," Terence said worriedly. "But now it's going to be impossible to stop!"

"Maybe it will just roll into a tree or something," said Beck.

"If we're lucky," said Angus.

"I think we'd better follow it!" cried

Tink. And the fairies leaped into the air to chase after the ball.

The cannonball was rolling fast now. It bounced across a tree root and rolled over a hillock of grass. It was headed for Havendish Stream.

"It's going to hit the mill!" cried Jerome.

This was truly a disaster. The mill was one of the most important places in Pixie Hollow. The tree-picking-talent fairies ground grains and nuts into baking flour there. And the dust-talent fairies used the mill to grind Mother Dove's feathers into fairy dust. It was also where the fairy dust was stored—all of it. An entire year's supply.

At once, the same picture flashed

through every fairy and sparrow man's mind: the mill smashed, the fairy dust inside blowing away with the wind. They would be unable to fly, unable to do magic. How would they even build another mill if they did not have the power of fairy dust?

A startled rabbit poked his head out of his burrow. But when he saw the cannonball rolling toward him, he quickly dove back inside.

The cannonball rolled over a large toadstool, flattening it. The fairies flew helplessly behind. They could hardly bring themselves to watch.

But just before it reached the mill, the cannonball hit a good-sized rock. It jumped into the air and changed course.

Instead of crashing into the mill, the ball splashed into the stream just above it. And there it stopped, wedged against the bank.

The fairies breathed sighs of relief all around. They laughed and hugged each other with joy. The mill was saved!

But Tink was not laughing. She did not take her eyes from the ball. As she watched, the water of Havendish Stream began to back up around it.

"Oh, no!" she said. "The stream is blocked!"

Everyone stared in disbelief. Tink was right. The ball had landed in the narrow branch of the stream that fed the mill. The water slowed to a trickle.

A few minnows had been thrown

from the stream by the force of the cannonball's splash. They lay flopping on the bank. With cries of alarm, the animal-talent fairies raced to help them. They scooped the little fish up in their hands and dropped them back in the water.

This was not good. Not good at all.

If the stream stopped running, the mill wheel would stop turning.

Indeed, they all heard the mill grind to a stop.

Rani started to cry, and it was not from happiness.

Why didn't I think of this? Tink asked herself angrily. *Why didn't it occur to me that once the ball started rolling, it was anybody's guess where it would end up?*

She sank down to the ground. She felt completely defeated. She had taken on a challenge that was too big. And she had failed. What was going to happen to Pixie Hollow now?

"Well, Tink," someone said. Tink looked up. Queen Clarion was standing next to her. "I guess it's time for you to come up with another idea," the queen said seriously.

This took Tink by surprise. She had thought the story was over. The ball was stuck in the stream. There was certainly no way to move it now.

But Rani was nodding and smiling through her tears. "We know you can figure this out, Tink," she said. "Look how many things you've already thought of. There has to be one more thing."

Tink was astounded. Not only did the others have hope that the problem could be solved, they thought she could solve it.

Rani is right, she thought. *There has to be one more thing.* Tink knew she had a responsibility to figure out what that one thing was. The other fairies were counting on her.

"Yes, Tink," said Florian. "It's time for your next idea. Do you want us to leave you alone?"

"Or would you like some nice soup while you think?" said one of the cooking-talent fairies, who specialized in cucumber soup.

"No soup," Tink said, squaring her shoulders. "I'm just going to think."

9

TINK FLITTED around the whole terrible scene, trying to focus. It was hard looking at the mess the cannonball had made. Water was starting to flood the banks of the stream, turning them into muddy pools. Toadstools and wildflowers had been squashed and flattened when the ball rolled over them. The cannonball had also plowed through a pile of acorns that the tree-picking-talent fairies had set aside to be ground in the mill. Now little chips of acorn littered the landscape.

Tink stared at them. They reminded her of something.

Little chips of acorn, she thought. *Little chips . . .*

"I've got it!" she hollered. "I've got the solution! I was thinking about it the wrong way the whole time! The cannonball is a huge thing, right?" said Tink. "It was much too heavy for us to move. And we certainly couldn't control it once it started moving. But even if we can't move a huge thing, we can move lots of *little* things."

Queen Ree nodded her head in understanding. "Of course!" she said.

"Of course *what?*" said a few fairies who hadn't caught on.

"We're going to break the cannonball into lots of tiny pieces and move them out of Pixie Hollow," Tink declared.

"Spring!" She turned to the message-talent fairy. "Ask the other pots-and-pans fairies to bring all the hammers and chisels they have in their workshops. And the carpenter-talent fairies—they have hammers and chisels, too!"

"I have a couple of chisels," said an art-talent fairy. "For making sculptures."

"Great!" said Tink. "Let's round up all the tools we have. We're going to break this cannonball up!"

A short time later, an array of tools was laid out on the grass next to the cannonball. The sand-sorting-talent fairies had piled sandbags around the ball, to hold back the stream. That way, the fairies wouldn't get wet as they worked.

Tink grabbed a hammer and chisel and flew to the top of the cannonball. As the best pots-and-pans fairy in Pixie Hollow, Tink knew a lot about metal. For example, she knew that every piece of metal had a weak point.

She put her ear close to the cannonball. Then she began to tap it with her hammer, inching across the surface.

Bing, bing, bing, bing, bing, bing, bing, bing, bing, bing, bong, bing . . .

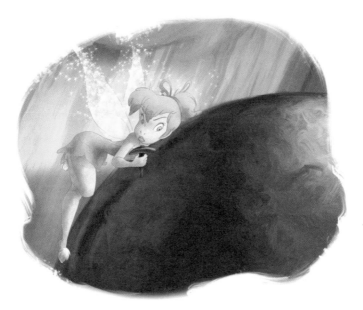

Tink stopped. She went back and tapped the spot again.

Bong!

Tink had found the cannonball's weak spot. Holding the tip of her chisel against the ball, Tink whacked it with the hammer as hard as she could. A crack appeared.

Tink whacked it again. The crack grew.

"Everybody take a hammer and chisel!" Tink told the other fairies. "Even if your talent is completely unrelated to breaking up cannonballs, give it a try. You might like it."

The fairies got to work. As they wedged their chisels into the iron, more cracks appeared. The air started to ring with the sound of metal banging into metal. It was a sound Tink loved with all her heart.

"I like this!" said one of the cooking-talent fairies, whose specialty was making ice sculptures. "It's just like chipping ice. But you don't have to be careful!"

Gradually, the cracks in the cannonball grew. Pieces began to break off.

The fairies laid them on the bank of Havendish Stream.

Soon they had broken the whole cannonball apart. A mound of iron bits sat by the stream.

"What are we going to do with all this?" said Twire, a scrap-metal-recovery-talent fairy. "It's more iron than we could use in an entire year in Pixie Hollow."

Tink nodded. But she wasn't really focused on what Twire was saying. She was getting another idea.

Quietly, she waved Terence over. "I want to ask your opinion about something," she said. "About fairy-dust magic." She whispered her idea into Terence's ear.

Terence scratched his head thoughtfully.

"I think it can be done," he said finally. "It will take a great deal of fairy dust. And the magic won't be easy. We'll have to concentrate. But I think it could work."

"That's what I hoped," said Tink.

She flew back to where the other fairies were still working. They were almost finished breaking apart the cannonball.

Tink stood on one of the bigger pieces of iron to make her announcement.

"Fairies," she said, "we're going to get this cannonball out of Pixie Hollow once and for all."

The fairies cheered.

"But what are we going to do with it?" asked Rani.

Tink smiled and said with a wink, "We're going to give it back to Captain Hook, of course."

10

SHOUTING WITH GLEE, the fairies gathered up the pieces of cannonball. There were many more pieces than there were fairies. So each fairy took as many as she could fly with. Gwinn took one big piece. Cedar took six small ones. Tink herself carried three pieces, and it took all her strength to lift off.

Meanwhile, Jerome and Terence were

inside the mill filling sacks full of fairy dust, as much as they could carry.

When everything was ready, the fairies lifted into the air. It was quite a sight, for those who could see it: a great cloud of fairies flying over the lush landscape of Never Land, headed for Pirate Cove. Of course, the pirates themselves could not see the fairies, who were invisible to them. If Captain Hook had looked up just then, he would have seen hundreds of chips of iron miraculously bobbing through the air.

But Captain Hook was not looking up. As the fairies approached the cove, they could see the vile-tempered pirate rowing a small boat through the water near the shore. He was muttering to himself.

"I'll teach that ridiculous boy a lesson," he growled. "Throw my best cutlass into the sea, will he? Thinks he can get the best of me, does he? Well, we'll see about that, Master Peter Pan. Let's see how you like a cannonball for your dinner tonight."

As Hook rowed, he looked down through the shallow water. Evidently, he was trying to find his lost cutlass.

The fairies were right above Hook's little rowboat. They hovered there, still in a cloud. "Okay!" Tink cried. "Start bringing the pieces together!"

The fairies flew nearer to each other. They began to fit the pieces of cannonball together.

"Now the fairy dust!" Tink commanded.

Terence and the other dust-talent fairies and sparrow men began to throw handfuls of fairy dust over the ball. Magically, the iron chips snapped into place like pieces of a jigsaw puzzle. The fairies concentrated, using all the magic they could muster.

In moments, the cannonball was complete. It was just as it had been when it crashed into Pixie Hollow.

And, of course, once it was whole, it was too heavy for the fairies to hold any longer. It fell from their grasp and plummeted toward Captain Hook's rowboat.

Hook looked up just in time to see a cannonball fall from thin air.

"What—" was all he had time to say before the ball crashed into the floor of

his rowboat. It broke through the wood and fell to the bottom of the sea.

At once, the boat filled with water. Hook had no choice but to abandon ship. He swam to shore as the rowboat slowly sank.

The sun was setting as the fairies flew back to Pixie Hollow, glad to finally be rid of the cannonball.

The next day, Pixie Hollow had just about returned to normal. Havendish Stream flowed between its banks, which looked none the worse for wear. The mill was turning once again. And fairies from several different talents had pitched in to help repair the courtyard.

The cooking-talent fairies had spent the day making acorn soup, muffins, cookies, and bread with the acorns that had been smashed by the cannonball. Everyone was good and sick of acorns. But all the broken ones had been just about used up, and nothing had gone to waste.

After her wet night in Rani's room, Tink had decided to sleep outside until her room was rebuilt. She'd found a nook between two branches where she would be sheltered from the wind and safe from owls. She had actually been quite happy out there, looking at the stars through the leaves of the Home Tree.

And in the morning, what had she

found by the roots of a nearby tree but her loaf-pan bed! It had one big dent in it. *Challenging to fix*, Tink thought. *But not too challenging.*

Later that day, Gwinn and Cedar helped Tink carry the bed up to her new room. They had worked all night to get it ready for her.

When Gwinn opened the door, Tink was speechless with delight. Her new room had colander lamps just like the old ones. The walls were painted with silver paint to make them look as if they were made of tin. And best of all, Bess had manged to finish a new painting for Tink after all. It was another still life of a stockpot, whisk, and griddle—and it was twice the size of the old one.

"It's beautiful," she managed to say at last.

Gwinn and Cedar helped Tink put her bed back into place. Then Gwinn took another look around the room. "You know," she said thoughtfully, "we could decorate with tiny cannonballs, Tink. So you'd always remember your greatest challenge."

"It's an interesting thought," said Tink. "But I'm all through with cannon-balls."

Just then, Dulcie came hurrying up to Tink's room. She poked her head in the open door and waved a metal sheet.

"Tink," she said, "do you think you could fix this baking sheet for me? I have one last batch of acorn cookies to put in the oven. It just has a little hole. I know it's hardly worth your attention. Not much of a challenge."

"Believe me," said Tink, "that is just fine with me."

And taking the sheet from Dulcie's hands, she headed for her workshop, whistling.

This is the end of
TINKER BELL TAKES CHARGE.

Turn the page to read
IRIDESSA, LOST AT SEA.

Iridessa, Lost at Sea

at

Sea

WRITTEN BY
LISA PAPADEMETRIOU

ILLUSTRATED BY
DENISE SHIMABUKURO & DOUG BALL

RANDOM HOUSE  NEW YORK

1

Iᴅɪᴅᴇssᴀ ʜᴜᴍᴍᴇᴅ ᴛᴏ herself as she fluttered beneath the leaves of a large chestnut tree. She snapped her fingers, and sparks flew from her fingertips. The sparks twinkled briefly before they were snuffed out.

Iridessa was a light-talent fairy, and she was practicing for the Full Moon

Dance. Every time there was a full moon, the light-talent group performed an elaborate dance. All the other fairies and sparrow men came to watch the light talents swirl and spin, trailing streams of colorful sparks behind them.

The next full moon was still many nights away. Most light-talent fairies hadn't even begun practicing for the dance. But Iridessa wanted to be absolutely perfect. That was why she was already hard at work, rehearsing her part of the dance.

Iridessa spun through the air, then stopped short. She turned to watch the trail of sparkles fade into the darkness behind her. It wasn't exactly even—three sparkles had escaped from the line.

Many fairies wouldn't have noticed the wayward sparkles, but Iridessa did. She sighed. "Not quite perfect," she muttered. "Yet."

She was about to start again when she heard a flutter and a low hoot. Something with large wings flapped overhead.

Without thinking, Iridessa dove for shelter in a nearby bush. "Ow!" she whispered. Thorns scratched her arm and ripped her dress. She tried to ignore them and ducked farther into the bush.

A breeze blew across her face. Then an owl landed next to the bush. A round yellow eye peered in at her.

Iridessa didn't breathe. She knew that some owls were friendly and wise. But some weren't.

The owl hooted again, and pecked at the bush with its sharp, curved beak. Iridessa's heart pounded in her ears. Now she was grateful for the thorns on the bush! The owl wouldn't be able to get past them. It hooted again.

But as Iridessa watched, the owl hunkered down outside the bush. It kept its fierce yellow eyes trained on her. Suddenly, she understood. It was going to wait her out. She was trapped!

Just then, Iridessa had an idea. With a snap of her fingers, she sent out a streak of blinding light. The owl hopped backward, surprised. Iridessa snapped another shower of sparks. The owl blinked twice. Then it flew away.

Iridessa stayed in the bush for

several long minutes. She listened for
the sound of beating wings. Finally, she
poked her head out of the bush. The
owl seemed to be gone.

Not looking back, Iridessa flew as
fast as she could. She didn't stop—she
didn't even slow down—until she
reached the warm, familiar lights of the
Home Tree.

"All-fairy meeting!" Iridessa shouted as
she flew down the hallway. "In the courtyard! Right away!"

Up and down the hall, sleepy fairies
fluttered out of their rooms.

Iridessa flew through each branch of
the Home Tree. She banged on doors

and sounded the alarm. By the time she reached the courtyard, it was packed with fairies and sparrow men. They looked tired. Many were grumbling.

Iridessa landed in the middle of the courtyard.

"What's going on?" someone called to her. "Why did you drag us out of bed?"

The fairies turned to face her, and a hush fell over the crowd.

Iridessa saw her friend Tinker Bell off to the side. Tink's arms were folded across her chest. She was tapping her foot impatiently.

"I was just attacked by an owl," Iridessa announced.

The fairies gasped.

"Attacked?" Tink repeated. "Are you sure the owl wasn't trying to be friendly?"

"We're sure," said a voice near the back. The animal-talent fairy Beck flew over and landed next to Iridessa. "Fawn and I tried to speak to the owl. We found its nest not ten frog-leaps from the Home Tree. But it wouldn't talk to us. The owl was completely wild."

The fairies buzzed with concern. A wild owl was a dangerous thing indeed. When wild owls saw fairies, they thought of them in the same way they thought of mice or moles—as a nice snack.

"Ten frog-leaps is too close," said a sparrow man named Chirp.

"So what are we going to do?" Tink asked. She loved solving problems. "Can we wait until it leaves, then move its nest?"

"Owls choose their nesting places carefully," Beck explained. "The owl would probably build another nest in the same tree."

Just then, Queen Clarion flew into the courtyard.

The queen looked around at the frightened fairies and sparrow men. "It seems we have a very serious problem," she said.

"We do, Your Majesty," Iridessa agreed. She blushed a little under the queen's steady gaze.

"We must find a way to make the owl move. What we need in this situation," the queen said, "is an organized fairy. Someone brave and clever to think of a way to get rid of the owl."

"That's exactly the kind of fairy we need," Iridessa said. Beck nodded. The fairies in the courtyard called out their agreement.

Maybe someone like Fira, Iridessa thought. *She's brave and clever. Or Rani, although she isn't very organized.*

"It seems to me that you, Iridessa, are the perfect fairy for the job," the queen finished.

"M-m-me?" Iridessa stammered.

"Good idea!" Beck said. She slapped Iridessa on the back. "Iridessa is the smartest, most organized fairy in Pixie Hollow!"

Iridessa was about to protest. But she looked out at the crowd of fairies and saw their eager, hopeful faces. Then she glanced at Queen Clarion. The queen was smiling at her. Iridessa swallowed hard. Even though she was afraid, she just couldn't say no.

"All right," Iridessa agreed. "I'll think of something."

2

Iʀɪᴅᴇssᴀ ꜰʀᴏᴡɴᴇᴅ ᴀᴛ the birch-bark
paper in front of her. She was sitting at
her desk with her chin on her hand. She
had barely slept all night. Instead, she
had been up trying to think of ways to
get rid of the owl.

There was a knock at Iridessa's door.
Without waiting for an invitation,

Tinker Bell popped her head inside.

"Tink! What are you doing here?" Iridessa asked. Tink was her friend, of course, but Iridessa had important work to do. She didn't have time for chitchat.

"Don't mind me!" Tink said. She opened the door all the way, and the scent of freshly baked cinnamon rolls wafted into the room. "Since you didn't come to breakfast, I brought you some of Dulcie's cinnamon-pecan rolls."

She placed a tray on Iridessa's desk. The tray held a pot of tea and a plate of sticky rolls dripping with gooey icing.

Iridessa blinked in surprise. She had missed breakfast? Iridessa had never skipped a meal before. In fact, she usually got to the tearoom early so that she could sit at her favorite table, the one closest to the kitchen. Whoever sat there was always the first to be served.

Iridessa's stomach gave a low rumble. She hadn't realized how hungry she was.

"Thanks, Tink," she said. It was nice of Tink to bring her breakfast. But Iridessa didn't usually eat sweet things in the morning. She always ate pumpkin-bread toast and a robin's egg omelet. Still, the cinnamon-pecan rolls smelled delicious!

"We have to keep your brain working!" Tink said.

"I could definitely use some help with that," Iridessa said. She poured herself a cup of tea and settled back into her chair. She waited for Tink to leave, but Tink didn't go anywhere. Instead, she perched at the foot of Iridessa's bed.

"Don't you have any ideas?" Tink asked.

Iridessa huffed in frustration and glanced at the list in front of her. "I have sixty-eight ideas," she said. "But I don't need sixty-eight ideas. I need one good idea."

"Maybe some of the ideas are better than you think," Tink said. "Read me your best one."

Iridessa looked at her doubtfully.

"What?" Tink demanded.

"Well, it's just that . . ." Iridessa tried to think of a nice way to say she didn't want Tink's help. It wasn't that there was anything wrong with Tink's ideas. It was just that Tink was a little too adventurous for Iridessa's taste. What if Iridessa didn't like her ideas?

"Well, you're not exactly a planning talent," Iridessa said finally.

"You aren't a planning-talent fairy, either," Tink pointed out.

Iridessa frowned. "All right," she said at last. One thing was clear—Tink wasn't going to leave until Iridessa shared an idea with her. "Here's number thirty-five. 'Surround the owl. Then make loud noises with leaf whistles and walnut drums to scare it away.'"

Tink pursed her lips. "That sounds dangerous."

"I know," Iridessa agreed. She crossed number thirty-five off her list.

"All right, what about number sixteen? 'Use smoke to drive the owl from the tree.'"

Tink shook her head. "Fire is hard to control."

Iridessa crossed that idea off her list, too. She read Tink a few more. Each one was either too dangerous, too silly, or just plain impossible.

"This isn't helping!" Iridessa crumpled the paper and tossed it into a corner of the room.

"Let me see that," Tink said. She picked the paper up and smoothed it out on Iridessa's neatly made bed.

Iridessa cleared her throat. Tink was mussing her blanket!

But Tink didn't notice. She was too

busy reading the paper. "What about this one?" she said. "Number twenty-one. 'Put a light in the tree so that the owl thinks it's always daytime.' That's a great idea! Owls only hunt when it's dark. All we have to do is figure out how to make a light. That should be easy. You're a light-talent fairy, after all."

Iridessa thought for a moment. "We could ask the fireflies and glowworms to help."

"They'll probably be afraid of the owl, too," Tink said. "Besides, even if we got every firefly in Pixie Hollow, their light wouldn't make it seem like day." Tink tugged on her bangs.

Iridessa took a bite of a cinnamon-pecan roll. "Maybe I could capture some sunbeams," she said slowly, "and put them in a bottle."

"Great idea!" Tink was so excited that her wings fluttered suddenly. She rose toward the ceiling.

Iridessa frowned. "But it would have to be a pretty big bottle."

Tink smiled brightly at her friend.

"So let's go out and get one!" she said.

Iridessa and Tink flew to the workshop of the glass-blowing-talent fairies. Most of the fairies and sparrow men were hard at work, but Melina took the time to answer their questions.

"Sure," said Melina. She led Tink and Iridessa through the glass-blowing workshop. "We have lots of bottles."

"Really?" Iridessa watched a fairy pull a long, hollow glass rod from a white-hot oven. The glass at the end of the rod was a half-melted blob of orange. Puffing her cheeks, the fairy blew on the cool end of the rod. The orange blob began to grow into a small sphere.

Melina caught Iridessa's glance. "Believe it or not, that's going to be a

beautiful vase. Ah! Here we are. Bottles."
Pulling off her work gloves, Melina
pointed to a shelf. "This is a big one,"
she said. She took down a red bottle the
size of an acorn.

Tink and Iridessa exchanged a look.
The bottle wouldn't hold very much
light.

"Um, do you have anything—
bigger?" Tink asked.

"Bigger than this?" Melina was
clearly surprised. "Well, as a matter of
fact, we do. The biggest this talent has
ever seen! To tell you the truth, we
weren't sure what we could use it for."

She flitted over to a wooden crate
and pulled off the top. Inside was a large,
round pale blue jug. It was nestled in a

soft cushion of clover flowers. "Isn't it enormous?" Melina said, taking it out.

Iridessa sighed. The bottle was about the size of a lemon—absolutely huge by fairy standards. But it wasn't nearly big enough for what she had in mind.

After thanking Melina, Tink and Iridessa flew outside.

"There's another idea to scratch off the list," Iridessa said miserably.

"There has to be a way to get a bigger bottle," Tink insisted.

"They don't exist," Iridessa said.

"Sure they do!" Tink replied. "I've seen them."

Iridessa frowned. "Where?" she demanded.

"In Captain Hook's quarters aboard the *Jolly Roger*," Tink said. "I noticed some when I was on an adventure with the Lost Boys."

Iridessa threw up her hands. "Tink, we don't need an adventure!" she exclaimed. "We need a plan." *That is so like Tinker Bell,* she thought. *To come up with the most impractical idea ever!*

Tink crossed her arms. "I'm just saying that there are bigger bottles right here in Never Land!"

"How in Never Land could we get a bottle from Captain Hook?" Iridessa snapped. "Just think about it!"

"I am thinking," Tink shot back. "Besides, it's not as if you have any better ideas!"

"Any idea would be better than yours!" Iridessa cried. "We've already got one problem, Tink. We don't need a hundred more!" Iridessa could feel her glow starting to turn red, the way it did when she was angry. "Are we supposed to ask Captain Hook for a bottle? Or swipe it out from under his nose?" Her voice dripped with sarcasm.

"Maybe I will," Tink said. Her blue eyes glinted dangerously.

"You do that." Angry tears sprang into Iridessa's eyes. Now she was back at square one. *I've wasted the whole morning with Tinker Bell,* she thought. *And I still don't have a plan!* "I'm going back to my room to work on some more ideas."

"Fine," Tink snapped.

"Fine," Iridessa snapped back.

And the two fairies flew off in different directions.

3

IRIDESSA WENT BACK to her room and halfheartedly scribbled down some new ideas. But she felt so terrible about her argument with Tink that she had trouble concentrating. Finally, she decided she should make up with Tink. After all, Tink had only been trying to help. Even if her idea about getting a bottle from

Captain Hook was silly, it wasn't much worse than some of Iridessa's own ideas.

She ran into Beck outside the Home Tree. "Have you seen Tink?" Iridessa asked. "I need to talk to her."

"Isn't she in her workshop?" Beck said. She looked at the teakettle where Tink fixed fairy pots and pans. It was unusually silent.

Iridessa shook her head. "I just checked. She wasn't there."

"That's funny." Beck perched on a toadstool. "I bumped into her a little while ago. She was in a hurry. She said she had to get something to help you with the owl problem. How's that coming, by the way?"

"Oh . . ." Iridessa waved her hand

vaguely. "It's fine." Her mind was racing. *Tink said she had to get something to help me?* she thought.

Part of their argument floated through Iridessa's mind. *"Are we supposed to ask Captain Hook for a bottle?"* Iridessa had said. *"Or swipe it out from under his nose?"*

"Maybe I will," Tink had replied.

A chill ran through Iridessa. "Beck," she said, "which way was Tink heading when you bumped into her?"

Beck thought it over. "Hmm," she said slowly. "I was herding the baby chipmunks back toward their nest. So I guess it must have been that way."

Iridessa gasped. Beck was pointing in the direction of Pirate Cove! "Oh, no!"

"What's wrong?" Beck asked. But Iridessa was already flying away, quick as the wind.

She knew just where Tink was headed—to the *Jolly Roger*, to get a giant bottle from the pirates.

I have to stop her! Iridessa thought. *Before it's too late!*

The *Jolly Roger* loomed like a mountain off the coast of Never Land. Iridessa was startled by its size.

How will I ever find Tink? she wondered. Anger squeezed her chest. *That is just like Tink—to flutter off to a pirate ship without a plan! She probably thinks it's another adventure!*

The wind turned in Iridessa's direction, and she was surprised to hear singing. She flew around the ship and peeked over the bow. A pirate with shaggy white hair was singing a cheery song as he mopped the deck. He wore a blue-and-white-striped shirt that strained over his belly. Another pirate with beady eyes sat nearby, coiling rope. His face was twisted in a sneer. With a shudder, Iridessa forced herself to scan the deck.

Tink was nowhere in sight.

Iridessa frowned. *Tink got herself into this mess,* she thought. *I should just let her get herself out!* But Iridessa didn't move. She was mad, but she was also scared for her friend. If the pirates caught Tink . . .

All right, Iridessa, think, think, think! she told herself. *Tink said she saw bottles in Captain Hook's quarters. So that's probably where she is.*

But where are the captain's quarters? Iridessa wondered. *Bottom, or top? Front, or back?* She didn't know anything about ships.

At that moment, a tall man in a long scarlet jacket stepped through a door. There could be no doubt that this was Captain Hook. His black curls spilled from under a wide three-cornered hat. He had a long mustache. And in the place where his left hand should be, there was a fierce-looking hook.

"Smee!" he bellowed.

"Yes, Captain?" Smee answered.

"Smee, I've finished my lunch," the captain announced. He walked up the steps to the front of the ship.

Now was her chance! Iridessa darted through the door. Behind her, Smee gave a snappy salute and said, "Aye, aye, Captain!"

Iridessa heard a clatter as soon as

she flew into the captain's quarters. Sure enough, there was Tinker Bell. She was struggling to lift a huge bottle made of clear glass. But it was too heavy for her. She had only managed to knock it over.

Iridessa flew to her friend's side. "Quick—hide!" she whispered.

"Dessa?" Tink's blue eyes widened at the sight of her friend. Heavy footsteps sounded outside the door.

"There's no time! Get in!" Iridessa said. She shoved Tink toward the bottle's open neck. Then she pulled a napkin over the bottle and climbed in after Tink. Under the napkin, she could just make out part of the room.

It was too dark under the napkin to see Tink's scowl, but Iridessa knew it was

there. "What do you think you're—?"

Iridessa shushed her. They heard a cheerful humming. Smee came into the room, and Iridessa watched as he shook his head.

"Oh, what a mess!" he said. He collected the dishes from Captain Hook's desk and dumped them onto the tray beside the bottle. "And we mustn't lose this!" Smee said as he popped the cork back into the bottle. The fairies felt the bottle rise into the air. Smee was carrying away Captain Hook's lunch tray!

Smee went out onto the deck, then down many flights of stairs to the kitchen in the belly of the ship. "Dear me, where has that cook got to now?" he muttered. "Ah, well. I'm the first mate, not a dishwasher. Let the kitchen boy take care of it!"

The humming and footsteps receded. The fairies waited for a few minutes. "It's all right," Tink said. "I think the kitchen is empty. We're safe."

Iridessa breathed a sigh of relief. "Great," she said. "Now let's get out of here—before someone comes back!"

4

Tɪɴᴋ ᴋɪᴄᴋᴇᴅ ᴀᴛ the cork, but it didn't budge. "It's stuck."

"What?" Iridessa's heart gave a flutter.

"It's stuck," Tink said again. "I can't get it out."

"Let me try," Iridessa said. She pulled Tink aside and tried to push the cork out of the bottle. It held fast.

"It's stuck," she told Tink.

"I just said that," Tink grumbled.

"Okay, let's think." Iridessa paced as well as she could at the bottom of the bottle. "Why don't we just fly?"

"While we're inside the bottle?" Tink asked.

"Sure! When we get back to Pixie Hollow, the other fairies can get the cork out." Iridessa fluttered up and placed her palms against the top of the bottle. "It's worth a try."

"Okay." Tink pressed her hands against the glass, too. "One . . . ," she said. "Two. Three!"

The two fairies fluttered with all their might. But the bottle didn't move.

Tink's face was pink with effort.

"Well," she puffed, "that . . . didn't . . . work. Got any more ideas?"

Iridessa strained to catch her breath. "What about you?" she shot back. "It's your fault we're stuck here!"

"My fault?" Tink cried. Now her glow turned pink, too.

"You're the one who had to get a bottle from Captain Hook!" Iridessa cried.

"Well, you're the one who thought of it!" Tink snapped.

Just then, the fairies heard footsteps again.

"Quick!" Tink said. She crouched and pressed her hands against the curved side of the bottle. "Push!"

Iridessa didn't have time to ask what they were doing. She just joined Tink and pushed. The bottle rolled forward, then stopped. It was stuck against the lip of the tray.

Behind them, the door creaked.

"Back up!" Tink commanded.

They did. The bottle rolled backward. And then, with a mighty rush, the two fairies rolled the bottle forward with as much force as they could. The bottle bounced over the edge of the tray. "Yay!" Iridessa cheered.

But the bottle kept rolling. "Whoa!" Iridessa cried. The napkin fell away, and she saw why they hadn't stopped. They were rolling down a chute. And the chute led right out a porthole!

"Stop!" Iridessa cried. But they couldn't stop. The fairies tumbled around inside the bottle as it dropped through the porthole.

Sploosh!

They landed in the water.

Right away, a wave washed over the bottle. Iridessa closed her eyes, sure this was the end. Once their wings got wet, they'd sink to the bottom of the sea.

But the bottle just bobbed to the surface.

"It's okay, Dessa," Tink said. She patted her friend on the back. "We're safe here."

Iridessa opened her eyes. The bottle was half in, half out of the water. On the other side of the glass, the sea was up to their waists. But inside, they were perfectly dry.

"I wouldn't exactly say we're safe," she muttered.

"Iridessa, look," Tink said. She crouched at the bottom of the bottle. A school of pretty blue and yellow Never minnows swam by. To the right, a silvery jellyfish with trailing purple tentacles floated peacefully.

Iridessa shut her eyes again. Looking at so much water was making her seasick. She was a very brave fairy, but she had her limits. "Stop watching the fish and help me think of a way out of here."

Tink stood up and checked the cork. "Maybe you could stand on my shoulders and try pushing it out again," she suggested.

Tink laced her fingers together to

give Iridessa a boost. "Wait," Iridessa said. "What will we do if I get the cork out of the bottle?"

Tink looked confused. "We'll fly away, of course."

"But what if a wave breaks over us before we can get out of the bottle?" Iridessa asked. "Our wings will get wet. We won't be able to fly back to shore."

Tink put her hands on her hips. "Are you saying we should give up?" she demanded.

"No," Iridessa replied. "I'm saying we need a plan."

"What we need," Tink shot back, "is to get out of here. That's the plan."

Iridessa rolled her eyes. *Some plan!*

"Would you quit worrying?" Tink

said. "Let's take this one problem at a time—starting with this cork!"

"Shhh!" Iridessa said. She strained her ears, trying to hear something out in the waves.

"Don't shush me," Tink snapped.

"Listen!" Iridessa said. "Do you hear that?"

The two fairies held perfectly still. Suddenly, Tink's face went pale. Iridessa knew that Tink had heard it, too—a steady *ticktock, ticktock.*

"What is it?" she asked Tink.

Tink slowly turned to look behind her. Iridessa followed her gaze—and found herself staring at a huge eye set in scaly green skin.

"It's the crocodile!" Tink cried, just

as the reptile's enormous snout opened
to show rows of sharp white teeth.

There was no escape! The fairies
watched in horror as the crocodile's jaws
closed around them.

5

"WHERE ARE WE?" Iridessa asked. She could barely make out Tink's face in the darkness. The only light came from their fairy glows.

Iridessa snapped her fingers and blew gently on the spark. The spark flickered, then grew into a bright light.

"We're *inside* the crocodile," Tink

said in awe. "He swallowed us whole!"

Iridessa looked around. The belly of the crocodile was full of strange objects. She spotted a brass candlestick, a teddy bear, a hairbrush, and a straw hat. "This crocodile will swallow anything," she remarked.

"Including that alarm clock," Tink said, pointing to the clock. It was red, with a round face. It let out a steady *ticktock, ticktock.*

"So that's where the sound comes from," Iridessa said.

Tink sat at the bottom of the bottle. "Yes. Peter Pan always said, 'To watch out for the croc, just listen for the clock.' It warns you when he's nearby."

"The warning didn't do us much

good," Iridessa said. She squeezed her eyes shut. A tiny silver tear trickled down her cheek.

Tink touched Iridessa's arm. "It's okay," she said. "We'll find a way out."

Despite her words, Iridessa could tell from the look on Tink's face that she was scared, too.

Suddenly, the bottle shifted and rolled forward.

"What's happening?" Iridessa cried.

"I don't know!" Tink yelled back.

The crocodile's jaws opened. Daylight poured in, along with a flood of seawater and an old boot. A second later, the crocodile shut his mouth and it was dark again.

The boot rushed toward the fairies.

It rammed against the bottle. "Hold on!" Tink yelled. The bottle spun.

"There's nothing to hold on to!" Iridessa cried. She braced her arms against the sides of the bottle as it crashed into something.

A deafening ring—like the sound of a hundred bells—filled the crocodile's belly.

"It's the alarm clock!" Tink shouted. "I think we set it off!"

The croc's belly gave a sudden lurch. His mouth opened, letting in daylight again. The bottle—and all the other junk in the crocodile's belly—floated toward the front of the crocodile's jaws. His mouth closed, and the bottle washed backward.

"I think he's got the hiccups," said Iridessa. She turned to look at the alarm clock. It had come to rest against the crocodile's side. The bells at the top of the clock were buzzing, tickling him.

The crocodile's belly lurched again. His mouth opened, and the bottle swept forward. But just when Iridessa thought they would wash out of the croc, the neck of the bottle banged into a row of white teeth. The crocodile's jaws snapped shut again. The bottle washed back toward the center of his belly.

"Quick, Tink!" Iridessa cried. "To the back of the bottle—I've got an idea!"

There was no time to explain. Tink and Iridessa rushed toward the rear of the bottle and pressed all their weight against its bottom. The neck popped up a little bit. Iridessa hoped that it was enough.

On the next hiccup, the bottle washed forward. But this time, they were ready. The neck of the bottle was tilted upward, just enough that the bottle floated past the croc's teeth—and right out of his mouth!

The crocodile looked at the bottle in surprise. Then his yellow eyes narrowed. He opened his jaws wide.

"He's going to swallow us again!" Iridessa cried.

Hiccup!

The crocodile hiccupped three times in a row. Each hiccup pushed the bottle farther out of his reach. Finally, with a snap of his enormous green tail, he turned and swam off.

The fairies sat very still, breathing hard. Iridessa blinked in the bright daylight. Overhead, three white seagulls glided past. The sky was a deep shade of blue.

A slow smile spread across Tink's face. "Well," she said, "that was some adventure, wasn't it?"

Iridessa couldn't believe what she was hearing. "Adventure?" she shouted. "You call that an adventure? We were eaten alive by a crocodile! And we're out in the middle of the sea!"

"We're not that far from shore," Tink said. She pointed into the distance. They could see a stretch of white sand

and green palms. "Something is bound to come along and help us."

Iridessa folded her arms across her chest. "Something—like what?"

"I have no idea," Tink said. "That's what makes it an adventure."

"You really are impossible!" Iridessa cried, throwing up her hands. "The only thing that will get us out of here is a good idea. And in order to think, I need quiet. So don't talk to me. You sit on that side of the bottle, and I'll sit on this one." Iridessa plopped herself down with her back to Tinker Bell.

"What am I supposed to do?" Tink asked.

"Anything you like," Iridessa said. She put her hands over her ears.

Tink sat down, too. Now the fairies were back to back. Tink started to hum a tune.

"I can't think while you're humming," Iridessa said through gritted teeth.

Tink sighed. She turned and looked at Iridessa over her shoulder. Finally,

she asked, "Do you have an idea yet?'

"No," Iridessa snapped.

"Oh, look!" Tink said. She jumped to her feet, making the bottle sway. "A turtle! Maybe he can help us!"

A turtle with a large hooked beak was swimming past them a few feet away. "Over here!" Tink shouted. She tapped against the glass.

"Over here!" Iridessa chimed in. She tried to get the turtle's attention by snapping and sending up a shower of tiny sparks.

The turtle turned slowly toward the fairies. He looked at them curiously.

"We need help!" Tink shouted through the glass. But the turtle just kept staring.

"Could you push us to shore?" Iridessa asked. "We're trying to get back to Never Land!"

The turtle was silent.

"He doesn't understand what we're saying," Iridessa said. *If only we had Fawn with us,* she thought, *or one of the other animal-talent fairies!*

"Help us!" Tink cried. She pounded her fist against the glass. "Help!"

But the turtle was already turning away.

"No!" Tink cried. "Don't go!"

As the turtle swam off, his rear flipper knocked the bottle. The shore in the distance grew smaller and smaller, while the bottle floated farther out to sea. . . .

6

THE BOTTLE HAD been bobbing along for hours. Across the water, the sun dipped to the horizon. The sky turned gold, then pink, then purple. Night fell, the moon rose, and the two fairies were still in the bottle, out at sea.

Tink stretched out on the bottom of the bottle and fell asleep. But Iridessa lay awake for a long time, looking up at the stars and trying to ignore Tink's snores. She couldn't stop thinking about the owl and the fairies in Pixie Hollow. The fairies would be safe tonight. They had scouts to watch out for the owl. But she knew that everyone must be wondering where they were.

Queen Clarion asked me to come up with a way to get rid of the owl, Iridessa thought miserably. *And instead, I disappeared! Everyone probably thinks I gave up and ran away.*

Iridessa sighed heavily. She had given her word that she would find a solution to the owl problem. And she had let everyone down.

Iridessa lay thinking most of the

night. At some point, she drifted off to sleep. When she opened her eyes, the clouds at the edge of the sky were glowing orange. All around the bottle, the water shimmered and twinkled. The sun was rising.

Tink sat up and rubbed her eyes. "Wow," she said when she saw the clouds. "Beautiful!"

Iridessa wished she could enjoy the view. But her heart was too heavy—and she was starting to feel hungry.

The sun was halfway up the sky when a white-capped wave came along. It pushed the bottle into a fast-moving current.

Tink leaned on her hands and knees, looking out the front of the bottle as they zipped along. A school of flying fish swam next to it. They shot into the air playfully and splashed down beside the bottle.

"We're finally getting somewhere!" Tink cried gleefully.

"Yeah, but where?" Iridessa asked.

"We're going to wash up on shore. See?" Tink said. "The beach is getting closer and— Oh, look, the fish are swimming away!" The school of fish darted suddenly to the right. Tink waved merrily.

"Tink!" Iridessa shouted. "Watch out!"

Both fairies let out a cry. Their bottle was headed straight for a giant rock! The current pounded against the rock, sending foam and spray into the air. The bottle would be smashed! Iridessa squeezed her eyes shut.

But the crash never came.

Iridessa opened one eye, then the other. She was startled to find herself face to face with a beautiful creature. The creature was as big as a Clumsy, but far lovelier. She had long, blue hair and eyes the color of pale violets. Iridessa looked down and saw that the creature had a fish's tail.

"A mermaid," Tink whispered.

Iridessa had heard stories about mermaids. She knew they were unkind and vain. Still, she thought the mermaid was very pretty.

The mermaid stared through the

glass at the fairies, her head cocked to one side.

"What has the sea brought us, Numi?" asked another mermaid in a voice as light and musical as a silver bell.

Another beautiful face peered over Numi's shoulder. This mermaid had brilliant green eyes—like spring leaves after rain—and yellow-green hair.

"It's a mystery," Numi said. She gave the bottle a slight shake. The fairies stumbled against the glass.

Iridessa tapped on the glass. "Miss Mermaid," she said politely, "we'd be grateful if you didn't do that."

Numi nearly dropped the bottle in surprise. "Oola, it talks!"

"Let me see," Oola said. She took

the bottle from her friend and frowned at the fairies. "Oh!" she cried. "I know what these are—they're fairies. I used to have one. But mine didn't have wings. And it didn't come in a glass cage."

"What did you do with it?" Numi asked.

Oola shrugged and handed the bottle back to Numi. "Nothing," she said. "It was very boring."

"Boring!" Tink squeaked indignantly.

"Hey! Hey!" Iridessa tapped on the glass. "We're not boring! If you let us out, we'll show you!"

Numi tossed her long, blue hair over one shoulder. "What can you do?" she asked.

Tink rolled her eyes. "Don't bother,

Iridessa," she said. "Mermaids don't care about anyone but themselves."

But Iridessa wasn't listening. She snapped her fingers, sending up a silver spark. Then she sent up another, and another. Soon the bottle was swirling with sparks.

"Oooooh," the mermaids said, their eyes wide.

Numi smiled. "Very pretty."

Oola frowned. "My fairy never did that."

"What can the other one do?" Numi asked. She turned her violet gaze toward Tinker Bell. Tink stuck out her tongue. She put her thumbs in her ears and waggled her fingers.

"Tink!" Iridessa nudged her friend.

"Stop that! Maybe they can help us!"

Numi giggled. "That one's funny!"

"I think she's rude. Let's get rid of her," Oola suggested. "But keep the other."

"Oh, I like them both!" Numi said brightly. "I could put the bottle by my bed. It would make a nice lamp."

"A lamp?" Iridessa cried. "Hey, no—wait! You need to let us out of here! We have to get back to Pixie Hollow to save the other fairies from an owl!"

"But then you'll fly away," Numi said reasonably.

"Well, of course we'll fly away!" said Iridessa. "Weren't you listening? We have to go help our friends."

"You fairies don't understand how lucky you are." Numi wagged a finger at them. "You're going to live at the bottom of the Mermaid Lagoon in a beautiful castle!"

Iridessa gasped. "B-b-bottom of the Mermaid Lagoon?" They would never escape from there! They couldn't possibly swim to the surface.

"We have to do something!" Tink whispered.

Iridessa nodded. The mermaids had liked her show of sparks. Maybe they would like something else that glittered. Beyond the rock, sunlight sent sparkles shimmering like diamonds over the water. Iridessa concentrated, drawing two sparkles together. Then three. Then four. Then three more. The sparkles joined like petals on a flower. They floated toward the rock, a water lily of light.

Oola scooped it up. "What is it?" she asked. Then she tucked the glittery flower into her hair. "Aren't I beautiful?"

Numi frowned. "Give me that," she said.

"Why?" Oola demanded.

"Because my fairy made it, that's why," Numi said.

"I won't," Oola said. "It would look silly in your hair, anyway."

"But it's mine!" Numi insisted. She reached for the glitter flower. And as she reached, she dropped the bottle.

Once again, the fairies landed in the water with a splash. But now they were on the other side of the rock, out of the current.

Gradually, the mermaids' argument faded into the distance behind them. Iridessa sat down next to her friend. "Tink, do you think they'll come after us?" she asked.

"No. They've probably forgotten us already," Tink said.

7

THE BLUE WATERS of the Mermaid Lagoon drifted into the distance. The bottle was bobbing out to sea again—this time in the wrong direction. It was headed away from Never Land.

"I'm hungry," Tink moaned. She and Iridessa sat facing each other. Their backs were pressed to the sides of the bottle. "I wonder what Dulcie served for lunch today."

Iridessa's stomach gave a low growl. "Probably mushroom tartlets," she said. Mushroom tartlets were one of her favorite dishes.

"Or cherry tomato soup," Tink suggested. "Or lemongrass salad."

"Maybe it was crab-apple sandwiches with mint sauce," Iridessa added. A shy flitterfish swam close to the bottle. Iridessa touched the glass, right where the fish's nose was, and it fluttered away in a swirl of bubbles.

"With honey cupcakes for dessert." Tink sighed at the thought of the sweet, crumbly treats, drizzled with fresh honey. "And rose-hip tea."

Iridessa rested her head against the glass. Until that moment, she hadn't realized just how thirsty she was. "We have to get out of this bottle," she said. A flicker of fear leaped in her heart. She didn't like the feeling. Light-talent fairies were usually warm-blooded and fiery— but now, Iridessa shivered. "If we don't get out soon . . ."

She didn't need to finish the sentence. Tink nodded. "I know."

If they didn't get out soon, they could be in real danger.

Suddenly, the bottle tipped and swayed. Iridessa looked up and saw a huge green wall of water. Before she had time to think, the wave crashed down over the bottle.

White foam swirled beneath them, and the bottle shot forward. The wave roared in their ears. Then, in an instant, the wave stretched out and quieted to a hiss. It washed them onto a clean stretch of white sand dotted with bubbly green seaweed. The wave retreated to the sea with a delicate swish.

Iridessa looked around. "Where are we?" she asked. In one direction, as far as she could see, white sand met blue water. In the other direction stood a lush forest. Tall, slender trees dripped with flowery green vines. Iridessa admired their pink-gold blossoms—she'd never seen such flowers before!

Tink grabbed her friend's arm. "Dessa," she said. "Did you see that?"

She pointed to something just over Iridessa's shoulder.

Iridessa turned to look. "It's just a hole in the sand," she said.

Tink narrowed her eyes at the hole. "Something moved," she whispered.

Sure enough, after a moment a long, spidery leg poked out of the hole, followed by a pretty shell. The shell was brilliant blue and looked like an oval stone. It was also very large.

"What is it?" Iridessa whispered back.

"I have no idea," Tink said.

The two fairies stood perfectly still, watching the shell. Another long, blue leg poked out, then two large pincers. Between the pincers was a small head with round black eyes, as shiny as ripe blackberry seeds. The creature was a crab.

"Hey, you!" Tink called to the crab.

Right away, the crab tucked himself back into his hole.

"I think he's afraid of us," Iridessa said. It was amazing that something with such large claws could be afraid of two fairies trapped in a bottle!

Tink's eyes were gleaming. "Yes—but he can help us! Hey!" she shouted. "Come back!"

"Stop shouting!" Iridessa cautioned. "You're scaring him!"

"Hey!" Tink shouted again. She pounded on the glass with her tiny fist.

Suddenly, a blue leg poked out of the hole.

The fairies looked at each other.

Tink tapped at the glass again. *Clink, clink, clink!*

Slowly, two antennas felt their way out from beneath the shell. Then the crab poked his head out. He looked at the fairies with his bright eyes.

Tink tapped lightly on the glass.

The crab scuttled closer on his long legs and waved a pincer, almost in greeting.

"It's okay," Tink said gently, tapping on the glass. "We're your friends."

The crab edged right up to the bottle. His beady eyes stared at it. Tink moved toward the bottle's neck, tapping all the way. "We need to get out of here," she begged the crab.

All at once, as if the crab understood, he clamped the cork in his giant pincer. With a twist and a pop, the cork came free.

Fresh air blew into the bottle. It smelled of the sea and of the pink-gold flowers. Air had never smelled as sweet to Iridessa. "Thank goodness!" she cried. She crawled out of the neck of the bottle and plopped down onto the sand. Then she gave her wings a huge stretch. They were stiff and sore.

"We're free!" Tink yelled. She followed Iridessa out of the bottle. She dropped next to the crab and planted a kiss on top of his blue shell. The crab began to scuttle away as she turned a somersault in the air.

Iridessa did a loop-the-loop. The wind against her face and her wings felt so good! Laughing, she darted toward the waves. She dipped a toe in, and then raced back to shore before the water caught her.

Tink stopped her somersaults and landed on the sand in front of Iridessa.

"Now all we have to do is get the bottle back to Pixie Hollow," she said. Her face was pink, and she was smiling.

Iridessa's smile vanished. She had forgotten that they couldn't just fly back to Pixie Hollow. They had to take the bottle with them!

"How are we going to do that?" she asked.

Tink gave her a huge grin. "I've got an idea."

8

Iridessa pushed the cork back into the bottle's neck. "I can't wait to hear this one," she muttered.

"Dessa, the answer is obvious!" Tink said. She waved a hand at the clear glass. "All we have to do is use the bottle as a boat. Look how far we've already traveled!"

Iridessa shuddered. "I'm not getting back in that bottle," she said. "No way."

"Not *in* it," Tink corrected. "*On* it. We'll ride it the way the pirates travel on their ship. It will be a fairy *Jolly Roger!*" Tink grabbed a twig and sketched her idea in the sand so that Iridessa could see. "We'll put the bottle on its side," she explained. "Then we'll tie floats to either side to keep it from spinning. We can use a stick as our mast."

"A mast?" Iridessa said. "What about a sail?"

Tink pointed to the forest behind Iridessa. The pink-gold flower vines were covered with large leaves. "There." Tink tugged on her bangs, thinking hard. "But what can we use for floats?"

Iridessa snapped her fingers, sending out a silver spark. "What about that seaweed on the shore?" she asked. "Each strand has lots of little air pockets in it."

"Iridessa, you're a genius!" Tink cried. "All right, I'll make the mast and the floats."

"What can I do?" Iridessa asked.

"Braid some rope," Tink said. "We're going to need lots."

The fairies got to work. Iridessa looked closely at the pink-gold flower vines and found that they were made of many slender tendrils. She yanked several down and started braiding them together.

Before long, she had a large pile of rope. She brought it to Tink, who was

weaving a thick mat of seaweed. Tink measured the rope. "We'll need more," she said.

"More?" Iridessa asked. But she went back to the forest to collect more vines.

By the time Iridessa returned, Tink had used the rope to tie the seaweed firmly to the bottle. She had crossed two big twigs to hold the leaf sail. Then she had used some sticky sap and a pinch of fairy dust to attach the sail to the bottle.

"It's beautiful!" Iridessa said.

Tink beamed proudly. "Not bad," she said, "considering neither one of us is a boat-making talent."

"It looks done," Iridessa said. She held out her rope. "So what's this for?"

Tink shrugged. "I don't know yet," she said.

Iridessa frowned. "You don't know yet?" She planted her hands on her hips. "I made all that rope for nothing?"

"Not for nothing," Tink told her. "I just don't know what for yet. But I once heard a pirate say that you can never have enough rope."

Iridessa's glow flared, but she forced herself to take a deep breath. After all, they didn't have time to argue. They had to get back to Pixie Hollow!

"All right," she said. "Let's get this boat into the water."

"I'll sit at the front," Tink said. "To navigate."

"What will I do?" Iridessa asked.

"Fly behind and steer," Tink said. "You'll have to push the boat in the right direction."

"Why do *I* get the hard job?" Iridessa demanded.

"Because *I* made the boat," Tink said.

"I made the rope!" Iridessa shot back. "We should take turns."

Tink gritted her teeth. "Fine."

"Who'll go first?" Iridessa asked. Just then, she noticed a flat white disk near Tink's feet. "We can flip this sand dollar," she said, lifting it out of the sand.

One side was perfectly smooth, and the other had a star pattern. "I call star," Tink said quickly.

Iridessa fluttered into the air, then tipped the sand dollar so that it tumbled down onto the sand. The sand dollar landed star side up.

"Star!" Tink shouted, leaping into the air. "I navigate first!"

Iridessa sighed. It figured. Since yesterday, she had been trapped in a bottle, swallowed by a crocodile, nearly kidnapped by mermaids, and cast away on a desert island, and now she had to push a bottle halfway to Never Land. She was starting to think her luck would never return.

9

TINK AND IRIDESSA struggled to get the
bottle back into the water. Time after
time, the fairies had to shoot high into
the air as a wave threatened to crash
down on them. Then they darted back
to the bottle to try again to haul it over
the waves. But once their bottle-raft was
safely past the breaking waves, a gust of

wind picked up behind them. The leaf sail puffed out as it caught the breeze.

Iridessa guided the bottle as she fluttered along behind it. *This isn't so hard,* she thought.

"More to the right!" Tink called from the bottle's neck.

Iridessa shoved her left shoulder against the bottle. It twisted slightly in the opposite direction.

"Perfect!" Tink cried. She gave Iridessa a huge smile over her shoulder.

Iridessa grinned back.

After a while, the fairies changed places. Riding at the front of the bottle was much better. When Iridessa was behind the large leaf sail, it was impossible to tell where she was going.

Now she could see land at the horizon. She saw tall white cliffs and a shimmering waterfall. Far to the left was a tiny speck of a ship—the *Jolly Roger*. If they stayed on course, they would reach the mouth of Havendish Stream. Then they could sail down the stream all the way to Pixie Hollow.

Sooner than she would have liked, it was time to trade places again. Iridessa noticed right away that the bottle seemed heavier than before.

She checked the mast. The leaf sail fluttered, then went limp.

"What happened?" Iridessa asked.

Tink flew to the top of the sail. She licked her finger and held it up to test the breeze. "The wind has died down," she said. "We'll have to push instead."

Iridessa strained her wings. The bottle was moving slowly. It was difficult to steer, too.

Suddenly, a wave knocked the bottle-boat off course. "Tink!" Iridessa cried. "Help!"

Tink flew to the back of the bottle, and the two fairies fought to turn the boat in the right direction. Once they had it back on course, they fluttered their wings like butterflies in a wind-storm. They pushed the bottle with all their strength.

Iridessa's wings ached. Drops of sweat broke out on her forehead. Her breath came in short gasps.

Tink and Iridessa had been struggling

along this way for several minutes when Tink noticed a strange shape swimming beside them. "It's that turtle!" she cried.

Iridessa stopped and turned to look where Tink was pointing. Sure enough, it was the turtle they had seen earlier.

"He's about to pass us," Iridessa said. Hot tears stung her eyes. "Tink, we're going too slowly. We'll never get back to Pixie Hollow in time!"

"I have an idea," Tink said. She flew to the base of the mast, where she had stored the rope. "He may not have helped us get out of the bottle. But he's going to help us get the bottle going!"

"What are you doing?" Iridessa called.

Tink had already tied one end of the

rope around the middle of the bottle. She made a loop at the other end, then flew to the turtle. She dropped the loop over his neck.

The rope between the turtle and the bottle stretched tight. It was working! The turtle was pulling them along toward Never Land. And he didn't seem to mind a bit. In fact, he didn't seem to notice.

Tink frowned. "We're still moving slowly," she said.

"True," Iridessa agreed. "But it's faster than we *were* going." A small smile twitched at the edge of her mouth. "And at least the rope came in handy."

Tink grinned. "I told you it would."

Iridessa tried not to watch the sky

as the turtle swam toward Never Land. She couldn't make the bottle move any faster. All she could do was be patient. She and Tink sat near the front of the bottle. The shores of Never Land grew larger as they got closer. After a while, a seagull wheeled overhead.

That's a good sign, Iridessa thought. *Seagulls like to stay near shore.* Soon they were close enough to hear the rumble of the surf.

"Tink," Iridessa said, "does it look as if the *Jolly Roger* is getting bigger?"

"Oh, nuts and bolts! That's just what I was thinking," Tink admitted. "It means our friend the turtle isn't going toward Havendish Stream."

Iridessa sighed. "I'm afraid we're

going to have to say good-bye, then," she said.

Tink flew to untie the turtle. "He's not the friendliest turtle I've ever met," she said as he swam off.

"The turtles in Havendish Stream are much nicer," Iridessa agreed.

"Speaking of Havendish Stream . . . ," Tink said, "we'd better get moving."

Both fairies flew to the back of the bottle. They pushed with all their strength. Luckily, the breeze picked up a bit, and soon the bottle was again sailing toward the shore.

"I see it!" Tink shouted. "I see Havendish Stream!"

The clear water of the stream sparkled where it met the edge of the

Mermaid Lagoon. Iridessa was happy that there were no mermaids in sight.

Her muscles ached, and she was more tired than she had ever been in her life. But they were close now! The bottle-raft bucked as they reached the breaking waves at the shore.

"We're almost there!" Iridessa shouted. She darted to the top of the sail. "Just a little to the left!"

Iridessa was about to rejoin Tink at the back, when a large wave crashed over the bottle. Instantly, Tink was soaked. She let out a choked cry as her wet wings dragged her into the sea.

"Tink!" Iridessa dove toward her friend. She grabbed Tink's outstretched hand and pulled her from the water.

Even though Iridessa was worn out, she found the energy to haul her friend onto the sand. The next wave pushed the bottle onto the beach a few feet away from them. Tink and Iridessa lay back, breathing hard. Finally, Tink spoke.

"Dessa," she said, "I can't fly."

Iridessa swallowed to clear the lump

in her throat. How could she make it all the way to Pixie Hollow alone? The bottle was too much for one fairy!

"Iridessa!" shouted a voice.

Looking up, Iridessa saw something flying toward her at top speed. She blinked. Was she sun-dazzled from too many hours at sea?

"Beck?" Iridessa croaked.

"I've been looking for you for two days!" Beck said. "You flew off so suddenly! And then when you and Tink didn't come home last night . . ." She turned to Tink. "You're all wet!" she cried.

"How did you find us?" Iridessa asked.

"A seagull spotted you. He said that

Tink was with you, too, and that you had some crazy boat bottle—" That was when Beck spotted the bottle-raft. She let out a whistle. "What have you been up to?"

Iridessa explained about the owl, the bottle, and the pirates. She left out the parts about the mermaids, the turtle, the deserted island, and the crocodile. *I can tell Beck about that later,* she thought. *When I have more time.*

"So we have to get this bottle back to Pixie Hollow," Iridessa finished up.

"Maybe you two can push it," Tink said. "With a little fairy dust to make it lighter."

"Push?" Beck shook her head. "That bottle is huge. I think we'll need help."

She put her fingers in her mouth and whistled. In a moment, the air was full of dragonflies. There were small purple ones, large golden ones, dragonflies with red and orange specks, and a few with golden stripes.

Beck spoke to them in a language Iridessa couldn't understand. They landed on the bottle in a swarm of silvery wings and pulled it out of the sand. They settled it gently on Havendish Stream.

Beck and Iridessa helped Tink on board, then climbed onto the bottle's neck. With a loud buzzing of dragonfly wings, they began speeding through the water.

10

IRIDESSA WATCHED THE scenery streak by
as the dragonflies pulled the bottle up-
stream. Tink opened her wings, drying
them in the breeze.

All at once, Iridessa realized that the
banks of the stream were crowded with
fairies and sparrow men. "There they
are!" shouted a voice. Everyone bubbled

with questions as the dragonflies slowed and brought the bottle to a stop by the side of the stream.

"What is that thing?"

"Does it have anything to do with the owl?"

"Iridessa! We thought the owl got you! It was back again last night!"

"Tink! Where have you been?"

"I'll explain everything," Iridessa promised. "But right now, I need your help." She pointed toward the bottle. "We're going to use this to scare the owl away." Her heart fluttered and she added, "I hope," under her breath.

In a flash, thirty fairies darted toward the bottle. It took only a moment for them to unfasten it from the floats and mast. "We need to pull out the cork!" Iridessa cried.

Beck called a woodchuck over. With a quick yank of the woodchuck's large teeth, the cork came free.

Raising her hands, Iridessa caught a brilliant beam of light from the setting sun. She placed it inside the bottle. Then she reached for another sunbeam. Fira saw what she was doing and came to help. Then Luna joined them. Soon all the light talents were collecting sunbeams and placing them inside the bottle as quickly as they could.

At last, the bottle was full. Beck pushed the cork into place.

The fairies had seen parties lit with fireflies and glowworms. They had seen moonlit nights full of stars. They had even seen bottled sunbeams. But they had never before seen a light as bright as this one. It seemed even brighter a few minutes later, when the sun dipped below the horizon. Around them, the forest began to grow dark.

Iridessa's eyes were just getting used to the twilight when a sparrow landed on a branch near Beck. She twittered, and Beck twittered back at her in Bird. "The owl has left its nest," Beck told the other fairies.

"We've got to get this light into the owl's tree," Iridessa said. "Before it comes back!"

Iridessa flew into the air. "This way!" she called. Behind her, fairies lifted the light-filled bottle and carried it to the owl's nesting tree.

They placed the bottle of sunbeams right beside the owl's nest. Then they bound it in place with strong spiderweb rope. The light shone in the tree as if someone had pulled the sun down to Never Land.

"Let's just hope it works," Iridessa whispered. She felt breathless.

"It has to," Tink said. Iridessa could see that her friend's lips were set in a firm line.

Just then, a fruit bat flew past, screeching a warning.

"The owl is coming back!" Beck warned. "Everyone, hide!"

The fairies vanished behind leaves

and into flowers that had closed up for the night. Tink and Iridessa ducked into a small knothole in a nearby tree branch.

The owl fluttered to the tree and sat there, blinking in the bright light. It settled in its nest and tucked its head beneath its wing. But almost right away it poked it out again.

The owl hooted unhappily. It tried to turn its back on the sunbeam bottle, but it was no use. The owl simply couldn't relax. It blinked at the light again in confusion. Then, with a mighty down-sweep of its large wings, the owl flew off.

For a moment, the forest was silent. Then a great cheer went up. All around, the fairies came out of their hiding places.

"We did it!" Iridessa cried.

Tink beamed. "Thanks to my great idea," she said.

"What?" Iridessa frowned. She planted her hands on her hips. "Don't you mean thanks to *my* great idea?"

Tink shrugged. "You helped," she said. She gave Iridessa an impish grin. "A little."

"Tinker Bell, you never would have gotten off the pirate ship if I hadn't come to rescue you!" Iridessa shot back.

"Sure—you rescued me," Tink said, rolling her eyes. "Right into the mouth of a crocodile!"

Iridessa giggled. "We got out again, didn't we?" she pointed out. "And I got the mermaids to let us go."

"That's true," Tink admitted. She smiled. "It sure was an adventure, wasn't it?" she said.

Iridessa shook her head. "Yes," she said at last. "It sure was an adventure."

Don't miss these upcoming
Disney Fairies collections!

Rani: Two Friendship Tales

Available in Fall 2010

Bess: Two Colorful Tales

Available in Spring 2011